Irving the Frog and His Violin

Irving the Frog and His Violin

Written By Michelle Zwirn
Illustrations by Nancy Lemon

I'm Irving the frog
And I love to play my violin
Atop my lily pad
In the pond we all call Friend

Irving the frog played his violin every day, upon his special lily pad in Friend Pond.

There he would sit, all alone in the small and tranquil pond, deep in the forest, and play his violin until the sun dipped below the earth.

Although Irving's passion was to play his violin, sometimes he felt lonely. Irving often imagined what it would be like to play his violin in front of a crowd of eager listeners.

One night, he dreamed about his many fans and how they came to Friend Pond just to hear him play his violin.

"Bravo, Bravo!" they chanted as they clapped their paws and stomped their feet. "More music, Irving, more music!" they demanded.

And, of course, Irving proudly played more music for his loyal and loving fans.

When Irving awoke and realized it was only a dream, he felt sad in his heart.

Irving was not aware that the deer, squirrels, birds, rabbits, bears, peacocks, owls, foxes, mice, and all of the forest animals loved his music.

He did not know that
Early in the morning, with the golden sunrise,
His beautiful violin music opens their eyes.
All through the day, into the late afternoon
They dance and play games to Irving's cheerful tunes.
And early in the evening, after the sun goes down,
His soft melodies help them go to Sleepy Town.

One day Irving wasn't feeling well. His mother, Mrs. Lilly Paddy, told him to stay in bed so he would get better. And even though Irving wanted so much to play his violin, he listened to his mother. Soon he was in a deep, restful sleep for the day.

That same morning, when the forest animals opened their eyes, they quickly noticed there was no violin music!

They became concerned and hurried to Friend Pond where Irving's lily pad floated without Irving atop.

"Where could Irving be?" asked Buddy Bunny. "He's always right here on his special lily pad."

The forest animals were worried about Irving. They scurried to his house at once. After three taps on Irving's soggy twig door, Mrs. Lilly Paddy appeared.

Very curious, Mrs. Paddy asked, "May I help you?"

"We hope so," replied a most sincere Whirley Squirrel.

"There's no music in the forest!" grumbled Burley Bear.

"Without Irving's beautiful violin music," squeaked Lizzy Mouse, "we cannot play all of our fun games!"

"That's right!" agreed Doe-a-Deer. "We dance and sing and play all day to Irving's fun tunes."

Mrs. Lilly Paddy was surprised as she announced to the pile of forest animals before her, "Irving never told me he had so many friends! I'm sorry to tell you that Irving is not well today so he cannot come out to play."

The forest animals could not bring themselves to mention that they did not personally know Irving. They did not want to admit they had never taken the time to thank Irving for sharing his music.

Disappointed, they started back to their homes. Just as they were about to go their separate ways, Spotty Owl shouted, "I've got it!"

"You've got what?" questioned Burley Bear.

"Here we are, feeling sorry for ourselves because we have no music while we play," Spotty Owl explained, "We should let Irving know how much we miss and love his beautiful music!"

"What do you have in mind?" asked Buddy Bunny.

As the forest animals huddled, Spotty Owl told them of his grand plan. They all agreed it was a great idea and went to work at once.

Meanwhile, Irving had slept soundly through the night. He awoke the next morning, feeling as good as new. Then he noticed hundreds of beautiful wildflowers all around his bedroom. He was surrounded by wildflowers of yellow, purple, green, blue, orange, and every other bright color of his imagination. Wildflowers that reminded him of the forest he longed to play in.

Irving's eyes followed the wildflowers around his room when he suddenly thought to ask, "Why are all these flowers in my room?" Then his eyes popped wide open as they fell upon a giant card in the shape of a violin. It was a get well card from all of the forest animals.

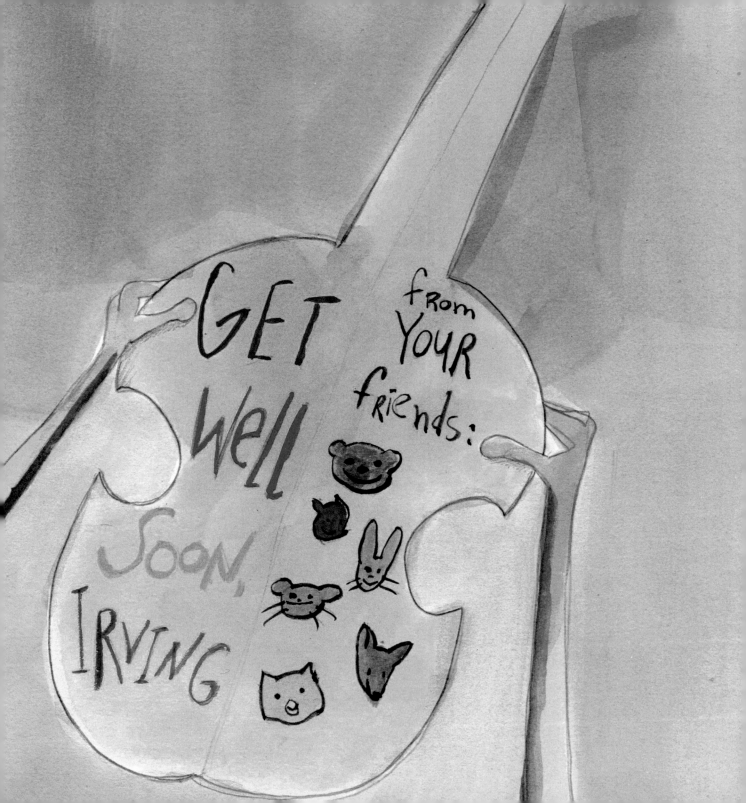

Dear Irving the frog,

You'd better get well very soon,
Because we like to wake up
To your early morning tunes.
We'll say it once more in another way
We love to hear your music all day.
And if we've never told you
At any time before,
We truly want to thank you
For your beautiful musical score!

From your loyal fans and friends of the forest.

Irving's heart was filled with joy! He thought he was all alone on Friend Pond where no one could hear as he played his violin. Irving never imagined that so many of the forest animals had grown to love his music.

The sun was just about to rise and shine through the forest. There was no time to waste! Irving hurried to the kitchen where he gulped down a bowl of Fly-Os cereal.

He snatched his violin and leaped quickly to Friend Pond.

Just as he landed on his special lily pad, he played the first musical note of the day. Then the sun rays shined through the trees as the dew sparkled on the leaves. And once again, the entire forest was enchanted by the soft early morning melody of Irving's violin.

Made in the USA
Middletown, DE
22 December 2016